The Stolen Horse

created by
Sharon M. Hart

written by
Sharon Dennis Wyeth

illustrated by
Sandy Rabinowitz

A
LITTLE APPLE
PAPERBACK

A Parachute Press Book

SCHOLASTIC INC.

New York   Toronto   London   Auckland   Sydney

cover illustration by Rudy Nappe

ISBN 0-590-41501-8

Copyright © 1988 by Parachute Press. All rights reserved.
Published by Scholastic Inc.
APPLE PAPERBACKS is a registered trademark of Scholastic Inc.

12 11 10 9 8 7 6 5 4   0 1 2 3/9

Printed in the U.S.A.   11
First Scholastic printing, October 1988

Contents

For my daughter Georgia,
with love

Chapter One

A New Arrival

"Look out!" cried Arden's big brother Tim. "A snake!"

Arden froze. A long gray snake slithered across their path, just missing her sneaker.

"Don't worry," Gran said. "He's harmless. Probably just on his way to the pond."

The snake slipped quickly into the forest, and Arden let herself breathe again. That's the way it always was when they were visiting their grandparents — never a dull moment! It was only nine o'clock in the morning, and Arden and her two brothers had already seen a trained bear, a baby elephant, and a snake! There were all kinds of interesting creatures at the River Oaks Animal Rescue Farm — not only the little ones that lived in the tropical forest, but the big ones that Gran and Gramp collected. Animals were the Quinn family business.

"Look what I found!" Jesse exclaimed, running back toward them. Seven-year-old Jesse was the youngest of the three Quinn children and a real explorer. He was always wandering off and coming back with something.

"A chameleon," Tim said. "Put it on that tree, Jess, so we can watch it change colors."

Jesse deposited the tiny, lizardlike creature on a tree trunk and his sister and brother huddled around to watch. The chameleon's green skin turned a light brown color.

"See?" said Tim. "Now it's the same color as the tree trunk."

"That's neat," said Jesse.

"Come on, everyone," said Gran.

"Let's keep moving. There are lots of chores to do this morning."

"When is Gramp coming home?" asked Jesse, hopping back onto the path.

"He should be along soon," Gran replied. "It was dawn when he left to take Simba back to the circus."

Arden and her brothers had said their good-byes to the gentle lioness the day before. Looking at the big, beautiful cat, it was hard to believe how near to death she'd been just two years ago when Gran and Gramp had taken her in. Only a veterinarian as skilled as Tansy Quinn could have helped her survive the terrible burns she'd suffered during the circus fire. But now Simba was finally well and on her way back to the big top.

Like the lioness, many other animals came to River Oaks to be treated and then returned to their owners. But sick animals and temporary boarders weren't the only ones Gran and Gramp took in. Some were homeless or needed a place to retire. And still others were endan-

3

gered species in need of protection. These Thomas and Tansy Quinn kept at River Oaks permanently.

Jesse ran up ahead again, and Gran asked Tim to go after him. "That turn near the clearing gets tricky," Gran warned. "You two boys wait for me there."

Arden watched her big brother dash down the trail. Lately Tim had gotten so tall that everybody said he looked a lot older than eleven. Arden wished that she would spurt up, too. She was small for her age and people were always mistaking her for eight years old, when in fact she was practically nine and a half.

"Thirsty?" Gran asked. "I've got some juice in my satchel. I know you're not used to this Florida heat."

"No, thanks," Arden told her. "I can wait to get a drink at the pump house." As they continued down the path, Arden looked all around her. River Oaks was so beautiful! The palms were bright green and there were pink and orange flowers everywhere. Wispy-looking Spanish moss dripped off the cypress trees, and the air had the wonderful smell of clover and oranges.

"Look there," Gran whispered. "An egret."

They stopped for a moment and looked up. Still as a statue, a great white bird with long black legs and yellow feet was roosting in a tree.

"Pretty, isn't it?" Gran said.

An unexpected lump rose in Arden's throat. For some reason the beautiful bird made her sad.

"Joanna should be here," Gran said matter-of-factly. "She'd probably love to photograph this one."

That was it! The egret reminded Arden of her mom's photographs. Last year Joanna Quinn had done a wonderful book of pictures — all on birds. There was one shot of an egret that Arden had found especially lovely.

Gran grabbed her hand lightly. "Homesick?"

"I guess I am," Arden admitted. It wasn't as if Mom and Dad hadn't left them in Florida before in order to go on one of their wildlife photography expeditions. But this trip was so much longer. And her parents were so far away — in Africa!

"A year's a long time not to see your mom and dad," Gran said quietly. "But it'll speed by like lightning — you'll see! But I hope it won't pass *too* quickly. I must confess I was kind of glad when we found out how long Walt and Joanna would be gone this time."

Arden gave her a puzzled look. "How come?"

Gran's sharp blue eyes twinkled behind her glasses. "Not too many grandparents get to spend a whole year with their grandchildren," she explained, giving Arden's thick brown ponytail a playful tug. "It's no secret that I think you're pretty special!"

Arden smiled. She thought Gran was special, too. Not only was Tansy Quinn pretty, but also she was really strong and could handle just about any animal. And she had a way with people. No matter how bad your problems were, you could be sure Gran would come up with a remedy.

"Throw yourself into things here at River Oaks," she told Arden now. "Find yourself a project and your homesickness will disappear in a wink!"

"You mean we can help you with the animals?" Arden asked.

"Yes, indeed!" Gran exclaimed. "With more than two hundred mouths to feed here, your Gramp and I welcome all the help we can get. Now, come on! Let's catch up with your brothers."

Gran's stride was so brisk that Arden almost had to run to keep up. In the clearing ahead, she could make out the bobbing of Jesse's bright red head. He was jumping up and down in excitement beneath a tall tree.

"Monkeys!" he called, pointing at the highest branches. "Come and see!"

Arden ran down the path to join her brothers. High above them were two pale-faced monkeys, a big one and a baby.

"Look at them go!" said Jesse as the acrobatic creatures swung by their tails through the branches.

" 'Morning, Happy!" Gran called, coming up fom behind. " 'Morning,

Chee-Chee!" She pulled a banana out of her bag and the larger monkey came scrambling down the tree trunk. The little one followed close behind.

"Say 'Thank you,' Happy," Gran instructed. The monkey squealed and took the fruit. Then she peeled it and broke off a piece for her baby.

"They're so cute!" Arden said, bending down to get a closer look.

"And they're clever, too," Gran added. "We actually rescued Happy from a ladies' room at an airport. When Gramp and I found her, she'd turned on all the faucets and was looking in the mirror, washing her face."

The kids laughed, and Tim leaned over to pet the little monkey. "Where did the baby come from?"

"Chee-Chee was born here," Gran explained. "The people who were shipping Happy didn't realize that she was expecting. But Gramp' and I could see it right away. When we told the owners, they asked us to keep her until the baby was born and old enough to fend for itself."

"Wow," said Tim. "I guess every animal at River Oaks has a story."

"Hey, look," Jesse said. "There's Gramp."

Sure enough, through the trees, they could see Thomas Quinn's animal trailer rumbling up the driveway.

"You think he's brought any new animals back?" Tim asked.

"Knowing your grandfather, I wouldn't be at all surprised," Gran answered. "But there's only one way to find out for sure."

Tim, Jesse, and Arden sprinted after the trailer.

River Oaks already had camels, llamas, and an okapi. If their grandfather had gotten another animal, what would it be?

"Maybe it's a bear!" Tim yelled.

"Or maybe a tiger!" Jesse shouted.

The trailer had stopped in front of one of the stables. By the time the other Quinns got there, Gramp was standing near the back with Joey Ortega, one of the trainers who worked at River Oaks.

"Did you get another animal, Gramp?" Tim shouted, out of breath. "What is it?"

Thomas Quinn was too busy to answer. He and Joey had opened the trailer door and were guiding something out.

When the animal came into view, Arden caught her breath. "A horse!" She loved horses!

Arden slipped under the fence to get closer, but Gran reached out and grabbed her. "Stay back," Tansy Quinn commanded. "Keep your distance."

Arden obediently stepped back. But her initial delight in seeing the horse turned to shock when Gramp and Joey finally got the animal out of the trailer. Then Arden got a better look. The horse's dark coat was caked with mud! Its mane was wild and tangled, and it was so skinny Arden could practically count its ribs. But it was the streaks of dried blood on the horse's back and legs that brought tears to Arden's eyes.

Chapter Two

---◆---

The Wounded Filly

"What happened to that horse?" Arden exclaimed, rushing forward again.

"I told you to stay back," Gran said. "I don't want you getting kicked."

The pathetic-looking horse began to buck and rear wildly. Both Gramp and Joey had to hold her by the halter.

"It's all right, girl," Arden heard Gramp say, calming the animal. "No one's going to hurt you."

"Why is its back all cut up?" Jesse exclaimed.

"Look at that!" Tim gasped, as a trickle of fresh blood ran down the filly's one white foreleg.

"Do something, Gran," Arden cried. "Please! The poor thing's hurt!"

"Calm down, everyone," Gran said gently. "We'll get the whole story from your grandfather. You three stay back here, now."

Gran walked over to Gramp and Joey. Thomas Quinn was a big man and Joey Ortega was strong and wiry. But it took all their strength to keep the horse from bolting. The filly neighed shrilly and her dark eyes rolled. From the corner where she was standing, Arden could hear the horse breathing loudly.

She's terrified! Arden thought sympathetically. *She's been hurt and she doesn't know where she is!*

"Quiet now," Gramp cooed to the filly. "I don't know where you've been, but you're here now — and River Oaks is a pretty good place to be. We're going to give you some delicious oats and lots of fresh water. And we're even going to fix your cuts. You're going to like your new home — you'll see."

14

Little by little, the horse stopped struggling. Finally it stood in one spot, dripping with perspiration.

Gran shook her head sadly. "Poor little filly," she crooned. "Get a bucket of water, why don't you, Joey? Let's give her a few swallows and then rinse her off. She's worked up quite a lather, she's so excited."

"Yes, ma'am, Mrs. Quinn!" Joey answered. The trainer ran off to the stable.

"Where did she come from, Thomas?" Gran asked Gramp.

"I stopped at the auction house on my way back from the circus," he said, stroking the horse's neck. "She's all ours. I got her for fifty dollars."

"Fifty dollars!" Tim said. "That doesn't seem like very much to pay for a horse."

"It's dirt cheap," Gran sighed.

Gramp's weather-beaten face looked weary. "It was like they were giving her to me. You see, the meat man was going to buy her. She was on her way to the slaughter."

"To the slaughter!" Arden cried, running over. "You mean she was going to be killed?"

Gramp nodded. "I couldn't let that happen. You should have seen how desperate she was to break out of the paddock! This filly's got a lot of spirit."

"Indeed so," Gran agreed, examining the horse's back. "There's a fine animal underneath all this dirt and blood — a thoroughbred!"

"Could be," said Gramp. "Of course she didn't come with any papers. The auction house got her from a farmer, and that chap got her from someone else. Word has it that she might have been a racer once."

Arden looked at the horse's thin, wounded back and felt like crying. Racehorses were highly valued animals. They were usually spoiled and pampered and fed the best oats. How had this one ended up in such awful condition?

Joey came out of the stable and gave the horse some water. Then he dipped a sponge into the bucket.

"Should I cool her down a bit?" he asked.

"Why don't you get a stall ready instead?" Gran answered. "I can rinse her off. It'll give me a chance to examine some of those cuts."

"Are those whip marks?" Tim asked.

"Maybe," Gran said, looking the horse over. "But these marks here look like they come from barbed wire."

Arden's eyes got wider. "Barbed wire? How did that happen?"

"Who knows?" Gramp sighed, wiping the sweat from his forehead. "Maybe she was trying to escape and got tangled in it."

"But why didn't her owner untangle her?" Arden burst out. "What kind of person would starve their horse and let her get cut in barbed wire?"

Tim's green eyes flashed angrily. "A

dumb one!" he fumed. "That's no way to treat an animal!"

"I'll say!" Jesse agreed hotly. "That owner should be ashamed of himself!"

Thomas Quinn looked furious. "I've seen meanness toward animals all my life," he rumbled in a deep voice. "I never could understand it."

Suddenly the filly flinched and started moving. Gran had touched a sore spot. "Get out of the way!" she warned Arden and her brothers.

The three young Quinns stepped back and Gramp took a stronger hold on the halter.

"She's got a big cut on her rump," Gran explained. "Most of the others aren't as deep."

"What about the leg?" Gramp asked.

"Looks like a scrape to me," Gran answered. "It'll heal — it just needs a little time."

"Did you hear that, little lady?" Gramp said, soothing the horse. "You're going to be all right. Before we know

19

it, you'll be galloping across the fields."

Joey came out of the stable with a bucket of oats. When the horse saw the feed, she whinnied. But as soon as the trainer got close, instead of taking the feed, she kicked out.

"Hey!" Joey yelled, jumping out of the way. "She tried to kick me, and she's dumped over all the feed!"

"The one who fed her before may have been the one who beat her," Gramp said, holding on to the horse. "It'll take her a while to trust us."

"Are you okay, Joey?" Gran asked.

"Fine," the trainer mumbled.

"Take a break," Gran said kindly. "Mr. Quinn will bring the filly into the stable and give her some more feed. And I'll put some antiseptic on the cuts and bandage that foreleg."

Joey nodded as Gramp began to lead in the filly. A couple of times, the horse balked and gave him trouble, but Thomas Quinn was a very patient man. Each time, he'd speak to the animal softly and get her moving again.

From her place by the fence, Arden watched in admiration. Her grandfather had once been a professional trainer, and everyone said he had a real gift. There wasn't an animal in the world he couldn't communicate with.

Arden started to follow. "Can I go into the stable with you?"

"Not now," Gramp said. "She's too skittish."

"There are some cookies and juice in the satchel," Gran called over her shoulder. But while Tim and Jesse made a nosedive for the goodies, Arden just stood there looking after her grandparents and the horse.

"What do you think of the new filly?" asked Joey Ortega, ambling over.

Arden's eyes welled up with tears. "I think she's beautiful. It's a shame she's been so mistreated."

Joey shook his head and bent down to pick up the feed bucket. "Oh, the cuts on her back will heal, all right. It's her personality that'll be the problem. Mark my words, she'll be bad news! When a horse gets hit and hollered at, she forgets how to trust."

"But she'll change in time, won't she?" Arden asked. "She'll trust again someday?"

The trainer shrugged. "It'll take somebody special to help her do it. Believe me — it'll take a whole lot of time.

Arden peeked into the stable, where Gran was wrapping the filly's foreleg. *Maybe I can do it!* she thought. And suddenly Arden just *knew* she would teach the filly to trust again. After all, she understood horses — she loved them above all other animals. And if there was one thing Arden Quinn had lots of, it was time!

Chapter Three

The Kids Next Door

The next Sunday after breakfast Arden and her brothers were running through the pasture. Everywhere they looked, there were beautiful butterflies.

"Look at that one," Tim whispered. "It's as big as a bat!"

"Let me get it!" Jesse shouted.

"Don't hurt its wings!" Arden said just before Jesse stumbled and fell on his stomach.

Arden went tearing after the insect. "There it is!" she yelled as the yellow butterfly landed on some clover. Its bold black markings glittered in the sunlight.

"It's the biggest butterfly I've ever seen," she breathed, creeping up to it.

But suddenly she heard the sound of hoofbeats. She jerked around. "What was that?"

"Hey!" Jesse said. "You let the butterfly get away. It flew over that fence." He took off again and Arden looked after him. There, a few yards away on the other side of the fence, was another field and a fancy white house. A little boy in a spanking white suit was standing on the ground watching a blonde-haired girl prance around on horseback.

"What do you think you're doing?" Arden heard the blonde girl scream. In his eagerness to capture the butterfly, Jesse was already climbing the fence. "This is private property!"

Arden and Tim ran over.

"Sorry," Tim said, pulling Jesse off the fence. "Come on, Jess."

"I didn't mean anything by it," Jesse sputtered. "I was just going to catch the butterfly and come back."

"No trespassing!" the girl said, pulling her horse up. "My aunt hates strangers!"

"That's right!" the little boy on the ground piped up, sticking out his tongue. He was just about Jesse's age, but not nearly as polite!

"Cool your jets," Tim said angrily. "We're not going to climb your old fence."

Arden put an arm around Jesse. "We're not actually strangers," she explained, trying to patch things up. "I mean . . . we live right next door to you, with our grandparents."

The girl on the horse screwed up her face. "How come I've never seen you?"

"We just got here about two weeks ago," Arden answered. Then she introduced herself and her brothers.

"Well, I'm Tiffany Van Vreen," the girl said in a snooty voice. "And this is my horse Winsome."

"He's a nice-looking horse," said Arden, doing her best to be polite. The

Quinns hadn't met any other kids in the neighborhood, and she was sorry they'd gotten off on the wrong foot with their neighbors.

Tim peered at the boy on the other side of the fence. "What's your name?"

Again the boy stuck his tongue out.

"Don't be ridiculous, Tony!" Tiffany said sharply to the boy. "He's my little brother," she told them. "But he never talks to anyone. He's too stupid."

Arden and Tim gave each other a look. They would never have said such a mean thing about Jesse.

But Tony didn't seem to mind his sister's insult. He plopped down in the grass and caught a cricket. Then he pinched it and pulled its legs off.

"Yuk!" Jesse said. "Look what he's doing!"

"See what I mean?" said Tiffany. "He's really dumb." She got down off Winsome and leaned against the fence. "My aunt says your grandparents keep

28

wild animals over there. How can you stand it?"

"We love it," Tim said, and immediately began telling her about all the exciting animals at River Oaks. "We even have lions and tigers," Tim boasted. "And they aren't in cages, either. Our animals roam around freely, just the way they would in the wild!"

Tiffany looked horrified. "That's awful! My aunt is right — you're ruining the neighborhood! It isn't safe!"

"But it *is* safe!" Arden said quickly. She went on to explain how the really wild animals at River Oaks were kept in special enclosures, behind moats and deep ravines. "The only way anybody can get to them is through a special gate across the keeper's bridge," she told Tiffany and Tony. "And there's no way the wild animals could get to us. They can't jump over the moats or ravines. We can watch them from the other side and be perfectly safe!"

Tiffany looked as if she didn't believe a word Arden was saying. "Even if it *is* safe," she sneered, "I still couldn't stand it. I hate wild animals. I like horses."

"We have horses, too!" bragged Jesse.

"That's right," Tim chimed in. "A lot of old circus horses retire here at River Oaks."

"Oh, those horses aren't any good for riding," Tiffany said snobbishly. "You should have a *real* horse, like Winsome."

"We do!" Arden said. "We have a racehorse. My Gramp got it last week!"

Tiffany lifted an eyebrow. "A racehorse, huh? That must have been expensive."

"She only cost fifty dollars," Tim blurted out. "Gramp saved her from the slaughter."

Tiffany laughed. "That horse must be some old nag. I bet she's just a bag of bones. Your grandfather should have left her where she was."

"She may be skinny now," said Arden, "but we're going to fatten her up. Anyway, I don't think any horse should go to the slaughter."

Tiffany shrugged. "Why not? — if they're no good anymore!"

"This horse is plenty good!" Jesse protested.

"That's right!" said Arden. "As soon as our filly is stronger, she'll be good for riding."

"If you like riding on a nag," giggled Tiffany.

"She's not a nag!" Arden said. Now she was getting really mad. "She's a racehorse — and I bet she's just as fast as your horse!"

"Who says?" Tiffany snarled. "You probably don't even know what you're talking about."

"She does, too!" Tim piped up. "Arden's a good rider. She even won a medal once."

Tiffany looked jealous. "A medal,

31

huh? Well, that still doesn't mean your grandfather's horse isn't some kind of nag!"

Just then a skinny woman in a ruffled dress came out of the big white house. "Who are you talking to, Tiffany?" she called sharply. "You and Tony come inside this minute! It's time for your baths. We're going shopping."

"I don't want to take another bath!" Tony whined.

Tiffany put on a fake smile. "Coming, Auntie."

The Van Vreens turned to the house without saying good-bye. Tim, Jesse, and Arden headed back across the field.

"What a bunch of snobs!" said Tim. "Especially that girl, Tiffany!"

"I'll say!" Jesse agreed. "Some neighbors!"

Arden didn't say a word, but inside she was steaming. She couldn't believe how awful Tiffany had been about the new horse. It wasn't as if she'd even seen the filly!

As they got closer to the stable, the young Quinns saw Gran and Joey talking outside. The black filly was tethered in the nearby pasture to graze. Arden slowed up and stopped beside her.

It was barely a week since Gramp had brought the filly to River Oaks, but already her cuts were healing. And now that Joey had started grooming her daily, you could see what a fine-looking horse she'd soon be.

"You're not an old nag," Arden said, carefully approaching the animal. "You're a real pretty girl." She reached into her pocket for a piece of apple and held it out to the horse. The filly nipped at her fingers, but Arden tried again. "Take the apple, girl," she said gently. "You can trust me — "

"Arden!" Gran's voice rang out, "Don't feed the filly. She might bite you."

"No, she won't," Arden called back.

Gran strode over. "You heard me, young lady — that horse is much too skittish for you to be fooling around with. Now, come on back to the house. Isn't it your turn to help make lunch?"

"Oops, I forgot!" said Arden. She followed in her grandmother's brisk footsteps.

"You must have had a *very* nice morning," Gran said on the way back to the house. "I hear you met our very best friends in the world — the Van Vreens!"

Arden's mouth dropped open. "The Van Vreens are your best friends?"

Gran winked so that Arden could see she was making a joke. "If you think Tiffany and Tony are unpleasant," she said, "you should try dealing with their aunt. I'd rather be best friends with a bunch of alligators!"

Arden giggled. From her first meeting with Tiffany, she had to agree.

Chapter Four

Glory

"Who's going with me to the visitors' park?" Gramp asked at breakfast the next morning.

Tim gulped his juice. "I am! I want to see the baby goats."

"The goats are my job!" Jesse cried. "I put the milk into their bottles."

"You can still give them their bottles," said Tim. "I just want to draw a picture of them." He jumped up from the table and got his sketchbook. "I've already done a drawing of Happy and Chee-Chee and one of the llamas. I'm going to send the pictures to Mom and Dad."

Tim showed his book to Gran. "What a nice idea," she said, leafing through the pages. "These are wonderful."

Gramp turned to Arden. "How about you, Missy? Do you want to go to the visitors' park or are you off to the stable?"

"To the stable," Arden answered, scraping the last bit of oatmeal from her bowl and licking the spoon.

"Not again!" Jesse protested. "All you ever want to do is hang around the horses."

"Pretty soon she's going to smell like a horse," said Tim.

"Now, don't tease her," Gramp said kindly. "Joey tells me that Arden's been quite a help. She's turning into a real hand."

Arden got up and grabbed an apple. "I just like horses, that's all."

"Yeah," Jesse giggled, "especially Bad News."

Arden's face got hot. "Bad News" was what Joey Ortega had nicknamed the filly, and both Jesse and Tim thought it was very funny. Arden, however, thought it was awful. "Bad News isn't her real name!" she said, sticking her chin out.

"She hasn't got a real name," Tim chimed in, "because she doesn't have any papers. So we *have* to call her Bad News."

"No, we don't," said Arden. "We could find another name that fits her."

"As far as I'm concerned," said Gramp, "Bad News fits her pretty well. That filly almost chomped my hand off the other day when I was deworming her."

"She's calmed down a lot since then," Arden argued. "When I'm with her, she never does anything like that."

Gran looked stern. "Don't you go messing with that horse unless Joey's with you."

"I won't," said Arden. "At least not until she gets completely used to me. I certainly wouldn't ride her until then."

"Ride her?" Gramp said. "That filly's not riding material."

"I bet she could be," Arden said. "All I have to do is get her to trust me."

Gran looked doubtful. "That horse would have to go through an awful lot of changes before we'd let you on her. If you want to go riding, you take out Old Maria."

Arden sighed. "Okay, whatever you say. But if the filly ever does change — if I get her to trust me — then will you let me ride her? Please? I know I could handle her."

Gramp looked as if he could be convinced. "If that ever happens, we'll think about it," was all he said.

Arden grabbed a fistful of sugar lumps from the sideboard and hurried out the back door. At least she had gotten Gramp to say that much. She couldn't believe what a fuss her grandparents made every time she even mentioned the filly. After all, it wasn't as if the horse were a really wild animal. And Arden had been making a lot of progress, visiting the stable

every day to help Joey with the grooming. She gave the filly food and water —
and whenever Joey wasn't looking, Arden stood right next to the stall and
offered her apples. The filly still nipped at her fingers, but Arden was sure the
horse liked her company. Lately the filly had begun to neigh softly whenever Arden came near, and the day before she'd even given Arden a nuzzle.

When Arden got to the stable, she went straight to the horse. Joey had given the filly a stall in the back, because she still raised a ruckus at night.

"Hey, girl," Arden said softly.

The filly took a few steps forward and whinnied. Arden reached through the gate and touched her shiny black coat. The horse trembled a little.

"Don't be nervous," Arden told her, as she unlatched the gate and walked inside. "It's only me. I'm your friend."

Joey was nowhere to be seen, but the filly wasn't tied so Arden knew the trainer must be close by. She picked up a grooming brush and gently ran it through the jet-black mane.

"Your coat is getting a lot shinier," she whispered. "And you're putting on weight, too. Soon you'll be nice and plump."

The filly turned her head and nudged Arden affectionately.

Arden stroked the velvety nose. "You're a good girl. Your name's not Bad News. That's a stupid thing to call you. You should be called something beautiful."

The horse lowered her head and began to nip at her bandage. Though the scratches on her back had disappeared, the scrape on her foreleg hadn't completely healed yet.

Arden pushed the horse's head away. "Now, don't eat your bandages," she scolded playfully. "We've got plenty of hay and oats for you."

Tossing her head, the filly neighed restlessly. Her dark eyes looked toward the open door at the other end of the stable.

"I bet you'd like to run around a little," Arden said sympathetically. The filly was rarely left outside unless she was tethered.

The animal pawed the ground and sniffed at the air.

"Okay," Arden whispered, taking hold of the halter. "I guess it would be all right if we went for a little walk. But you've got to promise to be good now."

They started up the aisle past the other stalls.

"Hey, there!" Joey's voice rang out. "Miss Arden!"

Startled, Arden spun around, letting go of the halter. The skittish horse bolted through the open doorway.

"Oh, no!" Arden said. "Catch her, Joey!"

"Come back here, Bad News!" the trainer shouted.

The two of them ran after the horse, but the filly was too fast. Before they could stop her, she had jumped the paddock fence and was galloping up and down the pasture.

"I'm sorry," Arden sputtered. "I didn't mean to let her loose."

Out of breath, Joey leaned against the fence. "It's all right, Miss Arden. I know you didn't mean any harm. I just hope we can bring her back in. She's having an awfully good time out there."

Arden looked at the horse. "She sure is," she exclaimed. "Look at her go!"

The filly's black mane and tail were streaming in the wind as she galloped through the saw grass. Arden's heart beat loudly. "I never saw such a fast horse in my life."

"She loves to run, all right," Joey said. "I guess she really is a racer."

The filly stopped running for a moment and stood in the field with her head held high, her graceful body perfectly silhouetted against the bright sun.

"She's good-looking, too," Joey said appreciatively.

"She's glorious!" said Arden. "She's not Bad News to me. To me . . . she's Glory!"

The trainer rested a hand on Arden's shoulder, and his weather-beaten face crinkled into a smile. "Glory, eh? Nice name. I like it. Now, let's see about getting her in."

It took a while for Joey to coax Glory back to the paddock after her taste of freedom. It was actually Arden's whistle that lured the filly close enough for Joey to slip on the rope. But once the trainer had hold of her, the horse was no trouble. In fine spirits after her run, she seemed more than ready to trot back home for a feed.

"Get a bucket of water," Joey instructed Arden, as they led the filly into the stable.

"Right!" said Arden, grabbing a bucket and heading for the hose. She was so excited that she didn't even notice the man who had been standing near the window. Arden tripped over the hose and fell right into him.

"Oh!" she exclaimed, startled by the sight of an unexpected visitor. "I didn't see you."

The man was tall and wiry and casually dressed in gray work clothes. When he smiled and took off his cap, he looked kind of like Joey, only his hair was shorter and his eyes weren't as dark.

"I was watching you out there," the stranger said. "You've got a pretty good whistle. Where did you learn it?"

"From my dad," Arden answered.

Just then Joey appeared and greeted the man with a warm handshake. "Hey, Vince!" he said. "Come to get that saddle? It's in the back."

Vince nodded. "Yeah, I saw it. I was watching you out the window with that filly. Where'd you get her?"

"Mr. Quinn picked her up," Joey answered.

Vince scratched his head thoughtfully and gave Joey a puzzled look.

"What's wrong, Vince?" Joey asked. "Something the matter?"

Vince shrugged and turned away. "Naw, I guess not. It's just that horse . . . there's something about her. Yes, sir, something strange. . . ."

Arden suddenly shivered for no reason at all. And as she stooped down to fill up the bucket, she couldn't help wondering why the man was so interested in her horse.

While Joey took his friend to the office to get the saddle, Arden carried the water to Glory's stall. "Here, girl," she said. "You must be thirsty. That was quite a run you just had!"

The filly snorted and took a drink. Then Arden pulled a piece of apple from her pocket and held it out. This time Glory didn't nip at all as she gently took the fruit.

"That's a girl!" Arden crooned. "You don't want to bite me. You know how much I love you!"

Glory licked Arden's hand.

Chapter Five

—•—

Ready to Ride

Arden lifted the old straw from Glory's empty stall with a pitchfork, while Tim stood by with the wheelbarrow.

"How much longer do you think it'll be before you can ride Glory?" Tim asked her.

"I think she's ready to ride right now," Arden answered, "especially since she's getting new shoes today!"

Tim helped his sister stuff the dirty straw into the wheelbarrow. "Do you think Gramp will let you?"

"Sure," Arden said brightly. "He said he would as soon as Glory calmed down."

"He said he'd *think* about it," Tim reminded her.

"Same thing," said Arden. She grabbed the rake and quickly ran it over the dirt floor of the stall. "Let's hurry. Joey and Gramp will be back with Glory any minute now."

Suddenly a small pile of hay tumbled down from the rafters and landed on top of Tim's head. "Hey!" he complained. "That's not funny."

Tim and Arden looked up. Happy and Chee-Chee were playing in the hayloft. Tim had brought the monkeys with him to the stable.

"Look what they're doing!" Arden laughed as the monkeys busily began taking apart a big bale of hay.

"Stop that, girls!" Tim commanded. "Come down here!"

The two monkeys scampered down the rafters. "Jump aboard!" Tim said, pointing to the wheelbarrow. "Let's go for a ride!" Happy and Chee-Chee clambered right in, chattering excitedly.

"Back in a minute," Tim told Arden

as he pushed the wheelbarrow outside. "I'm going to dump the old straw out."

"Thanks," said Arden. She gathered up an armful of new straw and made a fresh bed for Glory. Then she filled the feeder with hay. "I know I'm going to ride Glory today," she said to herself. "Gramp has *got* to let me!"

"They're back!" shouted Tim, wheeling in the empty barrow. Both monkeys were now sitting on his shoulders. Arden ran outside to the trailer, where Gramp and Joey were just letting down the ramp.

"How are her shoes?" Arden burst out. "Are they okay? Did she like the blacksmith?"

"She was very cooperative," Gramp said.

"I knew she would be," Arden said, petting the horse. "She's always cooperative these days, aren't you, Glory?"

As Joey started to lead Glory toward the stable, Arden grabbed his arm.

"Aren't you going to let her try out her new shoes?" she said. "Why don't we let her walk around some?"

"Guess she could use some exercise," agreed Joey. "I'll take her into the ring."

Arden turned to her grandfather. "Glory's real good in the ring," she said eagerly. "Come and see, Gramp!"

Thomas Quinn gave Arden a knowing look and followed her over to the ring. Joey was already there, leading Glory around at a slow gait. The horse was calm and obedient.

"It's hard to believe she's the same animal we brought in here just a few weeks ago," Gramp said, rubbing his chin. "Joey's done a good job with her. And he told me what a help you've been in bringing her around."

Arden blushed. "All I did was talk to her," she said, not mentioning the part about the sugar and apples. "But now . . ." she said with a swallow, "I'd sure like to ride her."

Gramp sighed and looked at the horse.

Perfectly controlled, Glory stepped around the ring. "Let's see if you can walk her, first," Gramp said.

"Oh, boy!" said Arden. She hopped the fence into the ring and walked with the horse beside Joey. Then Joey stepped aside and gave her the rope.

"Come on, Glory," Arden coaxed. "Let's just take it easy."

As she proudly walked the filly around the ring, Arden stole a look at Gramp's face. She could tell he was impressed.

Suddenly from out of nowhere, Arden heard Jesse's voice, and then her little brother came tearing through the back field. "Hey, everybody!" he shouted. "Look what I caught!"

Everyone turned as Jesse bounded up to the ring. He was holding a long black snake. "Hey, Gramp! Hey, Joey! Lookit!"

Glory stopped dead in her tracks and snorted. "Stay back," Arden called. "She doesn't like it."

But in his excitement, Jesse wasn't listening and he kept running toward them. The long snake squirmed in his hands. Glory whinnied and stepped backward.

"The snake!" Tim yelled. "Drop it!"

Startled, Jesse dropped the snake right next to the ring. "What's the matter?" he said. "That kind's not poisonous."

"Look out," said Joey. The snake was slithering into the ring close to Glory's feet. The horse stomped and began to neigh shrilly.

"Calm down, girl," Arden cried, trying to control the filly. "It won't hurt you."

But it was too late. Glory was spooked. With a forceful turn, she broke away from Arden and began to rear up wildly. Gramp and Joey jumped into the ring to catch her.

"Get out of the way before you get hurt!" Gramp yelled, pushing Arden back.

"But I can ride her," Arden pleaded. "Just let her calm down some."

"Do as I say," Gramp commanded.

Trembling, Arden backed away from the ring.

Glory was only out of control for a few moments, but that was enough to convince Gramp. As Joey led the excited filly toward the stable, Thomas Quinn's face got very serious. "I don't want to catch you riding that horse," he said to Arden. "She's too unpredictable."

"But it was the snake," Arden said. "It could have happened to — "

Gramp turned toward her sternly. "Didn't you hear me, young lady? I said, *Stay off Glory!*"

Chapter Six

The Runaway Race

Tim came bursting into Arden's room. "How come you're still in your pajamas?" he exclaimed. "We're supposed to go to the Everglades with Gramp this morning."

"I'm not going," Arden said flatly. "I don't feel good."

Tim plopped down on the side of the bed. "Are you homesick again?"

Arden shook her head. "Nope. I just don't feel like going."

Jesse crept through the door. "I know what's the matter," he said softly. "You're sad about Glory. And it's all my fault."

"It isn't your fault," Arden sighed. "Lots of horses are spooked by snakes.

They don't like stuff under their feet. I just don't see why Gramp and Gran can't understand that it could have happened to any horse — not just Glory."

Gran knocked on the door and poked her head in. "Breakfast, everybody," she called cheerfully. "Your grandfather is already downstairs waiting."

"Arden's not coming," Tim said.

"Oh?" said Gran. "Gramp is going to take you over on one of those little airplanes. Don't tell me you're going to miss a ride on one of those."

"I'll go another time," Arden said.

"We'll probably see some alligators, too," Jesse added enthusiastically.

Arden rolled back onto her pillow. "I feel too awful to see any alligators."

Gran came over and felt her forehead. "No fever," she said. "What seems to be ailing you this morning?"

"I don't know," Arden mumbled.

"I think *I* do," Gran said gently. "You're disappointed about that horse."

"If only Gramp would have given

her another chance," Arden said, sitting up. "When Glory was calm, I could have — "

"We know your feelings on the subject, Arden," Gran interrupted her. "But your Gramp is a good judge of animals and he doesn't want you riding Glory. She still can't be trusted. Understand?"

"I guess so," Arden grumbled.

"I hope so," Gran said before she and the boys left the room.

The minute she was alone, Arden threw off the covers and jumped out of bed. *It isn't fair!* she thought. How could they judge Glory on that one little time? Arden hadn't even gotten a chance to saddle her up. And Gran was wrong about Glory — Arden knew it! But if everyone thought Glory couldn't be trusted, no one would ever ride her!

It just wasn't fair! Glory was a racer. She wanted to run! And Arden wanted to be with her when she did.

Arden quickly pulled on her blue jeans and boots. "Glory's a good horse," she muttered to herself. "And I'm going to prove it."

Tiptoeing past the kitchen, she left by the front door and circled round back to the stable. Luckily Joey was nowhere in sight. Arden headed straight for Glory's stall.

"I shouldn't be doing this, girl," she said to the horse. "But somebody's got to show them that you're not going to hurt anyone."

She quietly led the horse out of the stall and saddled her up. Glory stood calmly. "That's a good girl," Arden said, giving her a scratch between the ears. The filly whinnied with pleasure when Arden took her out the door and into the paddock.

Arden walked the horse for a long time, and, as she'd expected, Glory didn't give her any trouble. "Now, let's go for a ride," Arden whispered.

Glory tossed her mane and flicked her shiny black tail, and Arden noticed that the bandage had been removed from the filly's foreleg. There wasn't a trace of a scar. The milk-white foreleg had healed as smoothly as the filly's dark back. Arden got into the saddle and made a little noise with her tongue. Glory trotted out into the pasture.

The day was beautiful. The smell of wildflowers floated on the air, and the tall grass in the field swayed gently. A feeling of excitement filled Arden's whole body. At last, she was riding Glory! The horse's gait was smooth as silk. "I knew it," Arden whispered. "I knew we could ride together!"

Glory whinnied and began to trot faster. Arden gave in to the horse's rhythm. As the filly cantered and then began to gallop, Arden could feel the horse's spirit and power. She leaned forward and let Glory run. The whole world seemed to be one brilliant, blue sky. Arden felt as if she and the filly were really flying!

But suddenly something white and gleaming caught Arden's eye — the Van

Vreens' fence! Before Arden could react, Glory's hooves left the ground, and then horse and rider were sailing through the air! Arden held on to the reins for dear life.

"What do you think you're doing?!" an angry voice screamed. It was Tiffany Van Vreen. "Get out of here this minute!" she cried as Arden and Glory came down on the other side of the fence.

Tiffany and Winsome were out taking hurdles. In the blur of excitement, Arden could see Mrs. Van Vreen and some other women watching from the edge of the yard.

"Who's that other rider?" Mrs. Van Vreen shouted. "What's *she* doing here?"

Arden wanted to stop, wanted to apologize, but Glory had a mind of her own. The filly had already jumped into the fray with Winsome. Spurred on by the sight of Tiffany's horse in action, Glory was following the colt's lead. Neck to neck, the two horses cleared the hurdles.

"You dumbbell!" Tiffany snarled in midair. "You're messing everything up."

"I'm sorry," Arden shouted breathlessly, catching sight of Tiffany's angry face as Glory moved out and took the lead. Tiffany urged Winsome forward, and the two horses turned together at the end of the field.

Tiffany's eyes flashed with jealousy. "So you want to race, huh?" she challenged Arden. "Well, you asked for it!"

Tiffany dug her heels into Winsome's side, and the colt whinnied shrilly. This excited Glory even more. The two horses tore back down the field and toward the house, taking the jumps as one. But when they reached the front yard, Glory was out in front again. Arden's heart leaped into her throat as the horse jumped the hedges, her hooves grazing the tops. Glory kept running all the way to the Van Vreen's stable.

"Whoa, Glory!" Arden shouted, and the filly finally slowed down and came to a stop. "That's enough. The race is over."

"Fast horse," Arden heard someone say. She looked around, startled. Standing in the shadowy doorway of the stable was a familiar-looking man in gray overalls.

"Howdy," he said, stepping forward with a smile. "I'm Vince Shago, the trainer here at Terrabella. I saw you and your horse the other day when I was visiting Joey."

"I remember," said Arden.

Just then Tiffany and Winsome soared over the final hedge and came charging up to them. "Of all the stupid things!" Tiffany sputtered. "Who gave you permission to jump in here with that horse?"

"I couldn't help it," Arden apologized. "She's a racer and it's my first time out on her and when she saw your colt, I guess she — "

"That's no excuse!" Tiffany cut in. "You don't know how to ride. Where did you get that horse anyway? She probably doesn't even belong to you."

"She does, too!" Arden answered. "This is the racehorse I told you about, the one my grandfather bought."

"I don't believe you," Tiffany said spitefully. "The horse your grandfather bought is a nag. You said so yourself."

"No, *you* called her a nag," Arden reminded Tiffany.

"That's a good horse," Tiffany said grudgingly.

"She's top of the line," Vince Shago said, examining Glory.

Arden smiled proudly. "We've worked hard to get her in shape."

"When I saw her the other day that leg was bandaged," the trainer said. "I didn't realize she had a white foreleg. That's good luck, you know."

"What a ridiculous superstition!" muttered Tiffany.

"Get off my property at once!" a shrill voice suddenly screamed from behind them. Arden glanced over her shoulder to find Mrs. Van Vreen glaring at her. Tiffany's aunt looked mad as a hornet.

"If I were you, I'd get going now," Vince told Arden kindly.

"Yeah, get lost!" said Tiffany. "And you'd better not jump any more fences. You can go by the road."

Arden and Glory hightailed it down the driveway and made a right turn onto the road. The filly trotted calmly toward home as if nothing had happened.

"We almost got into a lot of trouble," Arden said. "But I guess you're still pretty proud of yourself." The filly tossed her head and sniffed the air. "I'm proud of you, too," Arden admitted. It had taken a while, but they'd had their very first ride together. And even if it was a little bumpy, Glory had won a race!

Vince Shago stood outside the stable for a long time, staring after Arden and Glory. "So the filly's got one white foreleg," he muttered to himself. "I *knew* she looked familiar. . . ."

Chapter Seven

The Big Surprise!

The next morning, Arden came into Tim and Jesse's room at the crack of dawn. "Wake up!" she said, nudging Tim.

"Leave me alone," Tim groaned.

Jesse sat up in bed and yawned. "What is it?"

"I want to surprise Gramp and Gran and I need your help. Get dressed." Jesse got right up and trailed off to the bathroom.

Tim's eyes popped open curiously. "What kind of surprise?" he asked, sitting up.

"It has to do with Glory," Arden whispered.

"Oh, no!" said Tim, crawling out of bed. "What did that horse do this time?"

"*She* didn't do anything," explained Arden. "*I* did — I rode her!"

Tim closed the door quickly. "Arden, you're going to get into a lot of trouble," he said. "What happened? Did she throw you or something?"

Arden shook her head. "She got a little excited for a while, but I handled her. It was great. Glory's the best horse I've ever known, Tim."

"What's the idea, closing the door?" said Jesse, coming back into the room.

"Arden rode Glory yesterday when we were at the Everglades," Tim said in a worried voice.

"But Gramp and Gran told you not to," said Jesse.

"You'd better hope they don't find out," said Tim.

Arden grinned. "You don't understand — I *want* them to find out. I can't sneak around riding Glory forever.

Someone is bound to see me. I've got to get Gran's and Gramp's permission."

"But they already told you not to ride her," Tim argued.

"They'll change their minds when they see me on her," Arden insisted. "They just want to make sure I can handle her. And after yesterday, I know I can."

"Are you going to tell them?" asked Jesse.

"No," Arden replied. "I'm going to *show* them. All we have to do is get them to the stable after breakfast. That's where I need your help. Just give me a few minutes to get Glory ready and then bring them down there. Glory and I will be in the paddock."

"All right," Tim agreed doubtfully. "I just hope your plan works."

Arden smiled. "It'll work. Once they see how well I can ride Glory, everything's going to be fine."

After bolting down her breakfast,

Arden rushed to the stable. She was counting on Tim and Jesse to keep their part of the bargain. Without even looking around for Joey, she ran to Glory's stall.

" 'Morning, girl," Arden said brightly. She groomed the horse as fast as she could and put on the saddle. "Come on! We're going for another ride," she said. "Only today, we're staying closer to home. All right?"

Glory nudged Arden's pocket, and she gave the horse some sugar. When they walked out into the paddock, Joey was lifting a big bag of oats off the back of his truck. "And where do you think you're going with that horse, Miss Arden?" he said.

Arden's face got red. "Just taking a ride."

Joey dropped the bag at his feet. "I can't let you do that, Miss. Your grandfather gave me strict instructions."

"Gramp is on his way down here

right now," Arden pleaded. "It's okay. I promise!"

"He knows about this?" Joey asked, not convinced.

"Sort of," Arden said. "I mean . . . he will. I just have to show — "

In the distance, she saw Jesse running toward them. She didn't have a moment to lose! She knew that Gran and Gramp must be on their way to the stable, too. "Come on, Glory," she said, jumping into the saddle. "Let's show them. Nothing fancy, now."

"Nice going!" Joey called from the sideline as they trotted around the paddock in circles. "You've got a real knack with that filly."

Jesse was just coming up to the stable, and further behind, Arden could make out Tim, Gran, and Gramp headed in the same direction. But they weren't alone.

"Arden! Arden!" Jesse cried, running up to the fence. "It's the Van Vreens! They just came over!"

Arden slowed down a little to take a look. Sure enough, walking with Gran and Gramp was the skinny woman Arden recognized as Tiffany's aunt. And trailing behind with Tim were Tiffany and little Tony. Arden's heart began to beat faster. What were the Van Vreens doing here?

"That's the beast," Mrs. Van Vreen called shrilly, as they came up closer. "That's the animal that destroyed my hedges!"

Arden stopped in the middle of the paddock. Mrs. Van Vreen kept coming toward her, pointing a long, bony finger. "My front garden is in a shambles because of that creature. I always said no good would come of you Quinns keeping all these wild animals."

"Glory's not a wild animal," Jesse protested.

"I'm sorry about the damage," Gran said, trying to smooth things over. "I'm sure it wasn't intentional."

"Intentional or not," Mrs. Van Vreen

71

said, "those hedges cost a fortune. Something will have to be done about them!"

Gramp crossed to Arden and Glory. "Get down off that horse," he said. Arden had rarely seen him look so angry.

Sweat broke out on Arden's forehead. "I was just trying . . . I was just trying to prove that Glory could — "

"You'll have plenty of time for explanations later," Gran broke in firmly. "For now, do as your grandfather says."

Arden got down slowly and Joey led Glory back to the stable. Arden had a sinking feeling inside. Everyone was looking at her.

Tiffany came up and stood next to Mrs. Van Vreen. "It's your own fault," the girl taunted Arden. "Whatever happens now — you deserve it!"

Chapter Eight

An Unexpected Punishment

Arden sat perched on the edge of the couch in the Quinns' front parlor. The Van Vreens were gone, but Arden's problems were far from over. Not only was she in hot water for disobeying Gramp and Gran, but she'd also gotten her grandparents in trouble.

"One thousand dollars!" Gramp fumed. "The woman's being totally unreasonable. There's no way that her hedges could be worth that much."

"That's the estimate her gardener gave her," Gran sighed. "There's nothing we can do. We have to pay it."

Gramp threw his hands up into the

73

air. "With what? Where are we going to get one thousand dollars, just like that?"

"Maybe we can squeeze it out of the budget," Gran said quietly. "I could cut some corners."

"We can't cut any more corners, Tansy," Gramp said. "We're up to our ears in feed bills as it is. And what with that new elephant — "

"What new elephant?" exclaimed Gran.

"The carnival over in Timberville is closing," Thomas Quinn mumbled. "I promised to take in old Anna. Nobody else wanted her."

"Oh, boy," Jesse said. "Another elephant!"

Tim nudged him with his elbow. "Quiet!" he hissed.

Gran folded her hands in her apron, while Gramp paced the floor. A big tear rolled down Arden's cheek. "I'm really sorry," she said softly.

"There's got to be a way out of this," Gran said. "When Mrs. Van Vreen cools off, maybe she'll come down on her price."

"I wouldn't count on it," Gramp said. "That woman's having a field day. She's been waiting a long time for the opportunity to prove the River Oaks animals a menace."

"That's ridiculous," Tim burst out. "Mrs. Van Vreen's stupid. She hates animals!"

"Yeah," said Jesse. "She's making a big thing out of nothing. Who cares about her hedges?"

"Hold on, boys," Gramp said. "No matter what we think of our neighbors, Arden did trespass on their property. Not to mention the fact that she rode Glory against our wishes." He shook his head and looked at Arden. She felt miserable.

"Let *me* pay for the hedges," Arden pleaded. "I can sell souvenirs in the visitors' park on the weekends. I'll do anything to make up for the trouble I've caused."

"I can open a pet-sitting service like I did back home," Tim said eagerly. "I used to get ten dollars a weekend. I could help raise the thousand dollars that way."

"I can put on a show with some of the animals, like Happy and Chee-Chee," Jesse said. "I'll charge everyone in the audience a dollar!"

Gramp's face softened. "Those are all good ideas," he said, "but I'm afraid your grandmother and I will have to foot this bill. One thousand dollars is a lot more money than you kids think."

"And Mrs. Van Vreen wants it right away," Gran said softly.

Arden hung her head in shame. "I'll pay you back every penny," she vowed. "I'll find a way to do it somehow."

"If only you hadn't ridden that horse," Gran said. "Why did you disobey us?"

Tears fell from Arden's eyes. "I had to!" she blurted out. "Glory was my *project!* She needed somebody to love her. I knew that if I kept trying, she would learn to trust me. She just needed some attention and. . . ." She hid her face in her hands.

Gran came over and touched the girl gently. "We're not faulting you for feeling sorry for the animal. But it's not only the hedges we're concerned about. You could have been hurt."

"Glory would never hurt me," Arden insisted. "She trusts me now. All I wanted was to prove it. I just wanted a chance to ride her. And Glory needed a chance, too. She wants to run — she's a racer! She — "

The shrill sound of the telephone cut off Arden's explanation. When Gran went to answer it, Gramp sat down next to Arden on the couch. "There, there . . ." he said, wiping away her tears with his handkerchief. "We know your heart was in the right place. I haven't been an animal keeper all these years for nothing."

A few minutes later Gran came back into the room. "I just had a very interesting call . . . from Mrs. Van Vreen."

"Now what does she want?" Gramp grumbled.

"She's offered us a way out," Gran answered.

"You mean we don't have to give her the money?" Arden asked, brightening up.

Gran looked away. "Not exactly."

"Out with it, Tansy," Gramp prompted. "What did the woman say?"

Gran crossed to the window. "It seems that Tiffany has taken a real shine to Glory. Mrs. Van Vreen said she'd forgive the damage to the hedges if we'd give her the horse."

"What did you say?" Arden gasped.

"What *could* I say?" Gran flushed. "The ·horse only cost us fifty dollars. It's a small price to pay in order to save a thousand."

"No!" Arden cried. "Please don't give her away!"

Gran looked at Gramp. "Your grandmother's right," Gramp said sadly. "We can't afford to refuse Mrs. Van Vreen's offer. Glory will have to go to Terrabella."

Chapter Nine

Letting Go

Arden sat still as a statue beneath a palm tree in the backyard. She didn't feel like doing anything. Following Gran's announcement that Glory would actually be going to the Van Vreens', she couldn't even bring herself to visit the stable. It was too hard. How could she look at Glory when she knew she'd never get to ride her again, knew she'd have to give her up?

"Look what I've got!" said Jesse, prancing into the yard with a mynah bird on his shoulder. "His name is Mortie," Jesse explained. "Gramp let me take him out of the bird shelter. He's really nice and he can talk!"

Arden gazed dully at Jesse and the bird. Any other time she would have been really interested.

"What's your name?" Jesse commanded, letting the bird hop onto his finger.

"My name is Mortie!" the mynah squawked.

"Did you hear that?" Jesse cried. "Neat, huh?"

"Yeah, neat . . ." Arden said softly.

"What a lovely day!" Mortie screeched.

Jesse grinned. "He's a really nice bird. Good boy, Mortie!"

"Good boy!" the bird repeated.

"Isn't he smart?" Jesse exclaimed. "I'm going to train him to say all kinds of things."

But the mynah already had his own vocabulary. "What's up, Stupid?" he suddenly cried.

Jesse's mouth dropped open.

"Give me a biscuit, Shorty!" the bird demanded.

Arden's eyes twinkled. "Nice bird, huh? He sounds like Tiffany Van Vreen. I hope *you* didn't teach him to talk like that."

"I never heard him say any of this stuff," Jesse declared. "Mind your manners, Mortie!" he scolded.

The mynah flapped his wings. "Mind your manners, Dog Face!"

"Who are you calling a dog face?" Jesse yelled. "Sorry," he said to Arden. "I didn't know he was so rude. I was just trying to cheer you up."

Arden giggled. "You did. Thanks."

"Come on, Mortie," Jesse said, walking away with the mynah. "I've got to teach you some manners."

A little later Gran and Gramp came out of the back door together. "You've been sitting under this tree for a long time," Gran said to Arden. "Guess you're feeling pretty bad about Glory."

"Yes, I am," Arden said. "But . . . but I understand."

"There are lots of animals besides Glory here at River Oaks," Gramp said gently. "We can't sacrifice the welfare of all of them for the sake of keeping one horse. That one thousand dollars Mrs. Van Vreen wanted can buy a lot of feed and medical supplies."

"I wish there was another way," Gran sighed. "But at least we know Glory will be going to a place where she'll be well cared for. The Van Vreens have a good stable, and Vince Shago is wonderful with horses."

Arden swallowed. She knew her grandparents were only doing what had to be done. The most important thing was to keep River Oaks going. "Glory would have been dead if Gramp hadn't bought her at the auction," she said. "I know you have to do what's right for *all* the animals."

"It's very grown-up of you to understand that," said Gramp. "And Gran and I understand how hard it is for you to give up an animal you love."

Gran stroked Arden's head. "We've told Mrs. Van Vreen that she can't have Glory until next week. We thought you might like some time with the horse before she goes to Terrabella."

"Have you been to the stable today?" Gramp asked.

Arden's lip began to tremble. "I haven't seen Glory since yesterday."

Gramp put his arm around Arden's shoulder. "Why don't we go down now? I'll take out Ruby and we'll saddle up Glory for you."

Arden's brown eyes filled with tears. "You mean I can ride her?"

Gramp nodded. "We'll go out together. After all, you never did get a chance to show me what you can do with the horse."

Arden's spirits began to lift. Glory was going to Terrabella, but not for another whole week. She *would* ride the filly again after all . . . and with Gramp right there beside her!

They waved good-bye to Gran and started toward the stable.

"No races now," Gramp said, taking her hand. "A horse as young as Glory should be paced carefully, especially after the bad start she had before she came here."

"Remember how skinny she was when we got her?" said Arden. "I guess her old owners would be pretty surprised to see how healthy she is now."

At the stable, they bumped into Tim with his sketchbook. "I thought you were feeding the monkeys," Gramp said.

"What are you doing here?"

Tim stole a look at Arden. "I'm . . . not doing anything," he said, putting the book behind his back. "I was just visiting the horses. See you later."

"Don't forget about those monkeys!" Gramp called after him.

Arden got a saddle and ran to Glory's stall. The filly let out a joyful whinny.

"Glory missed you," Gramp said.

"I missed her, too," said Arden. She felt a sudden pang, thinking of the day the horse would go to Terrabella.

"Get her ready," Gramp said gently. "I'll go fetch a saddle for Ruby. I can't wait to see what you and Glory can do."

"Maybe you can give us a few pointers," Arden called.

Gramp winked over his shoulder. "You bet!"

Minutes later Arden and Gramp were on their way. The horses took them along grassy paths and through the forests, where they spied on the zebras in their habitat and stopped at the pond to see the herons. They tromped across the farthest fields of River Oaks and along the canal. And through it all, Glory behaved beautifully. Gramp couldn't have been more impressed.

"I see what you mean about that horse," he said. "When she's with you, she's sweet as sugar."

Arden laughed mischievously. "I've fed her enough sugar — that's for sure!"

The afternoon was so much fun Arden wished it could go on forever. That night, before she went to sleep, she curled up in bed and began a letter to her parents.

Dear Mom and Dad, Arden wrote. *Sorry I haven't written in a while. I've been real busy with Glory. I finally got her to trust me! Today Gramp and I went riding all over River Oaks. . . .*

But Arden never finished the letter. She started crying when she got to the part about how she'd soon be telling the horse good-bye. Then she lay in bed for a long time, staring at the ceiling.

Down at the stable, Glory was still awake, too. And so was Joey. He was standing next to the filly's stall with Vince Shago.

"It finally came to me," Vince said. "I knew from the first that there was something about that horse. She's a dead ringer for Midnight Clear's foal! I was working at Wentworth Track and Stables when the foal was born there. She was a jet-black filly just like this one, with one white foreleg."

"What was the foal's name?" Joey asked.

Vince scratched his head. "That's the funny part. She was called Rappadan Glory."

"And this one is Arden's Glory," Joey said softly. "But what happened to the foal you used to know? Isn't she still over at Wentworth Stables?"

"No sir, she isn't. Midnight Clear's foal was stolen."

"Stolen!" Joey exclaimed. "How long ago was that?"

"I hear she's been missing about a year," Vince replied. "Wentworth always suspected the trainer who took my place of stealing the foal. This guy had a real nasty temper. Wentworth finally had to fire him!"

Joey crossed over to Glory's stall and stroked the horse on the nose. "If Glory's the horse you're talking about, that means she's stolen property. How are we going to find out for sure?"

Vince got up. "Jed Wentworth's the owner of Wentworth Stables. If it *is* his horse, you can be sure Jed will be able to identify her. Unfortunately, he'll be out of town until next week. But as soon as he gets back, I'll give him a call."

The two men left Glory's stall and walked outside. The only sound in the stable was the breathing of the animals. All of the horses except Glory were asleep. The filly stood in the middle of her stall staring into the darkness. Like Arden, she was wide awake.

Chapter Ten

Good-bye Glory?

On Glory's last morning at River Oaks, Arden got up at dawn. She watered and fed the horse, then groomed her carefully. *This is the last time I'll groom her!* she thought. *This is the last time we'll be together!* After today, Arden knew, she'd only be able to see Glory across a fence. From now on, her horse would be riding with someone else — with Tiffany!

Arden hugged the filly's neck. "I'm going to miss you, girl," she whispered. "Don't forget me!"

Suddenly Arden heard a noise.

"It's only me, Sis," Tim said, coming through the doorway.

Arden turned around. "I thought it might be the Van Vreens," she said quietly.

Tim was holding something behind his back.

"What have you got there?" Arden asked.

He thrust a drawing into her hand. "Here — you may not have the real Glory, but you can keep this forever."

It was a picture of Glory! Tim had drawn the filly with her mane blown back in the wind as if she were racing.

"It's beautiful, Tim," Arden said, hugging her brother. "Thank you!"

Just then Jesse peeked in from outside. "Those weirdo Van Vreens are here," he whispered.

Joey Ortega walked in, and Arden took a deep breath. "I'm sorry, Arden," the trainer told her. "It's time for Glory to go."

Arden gave the horse one last hug. "All right," she said, trying hard not to cry. "You can take her."

Joey took the horse's rope and led her to the door. Glory turned back to look at Arden.

"It's okay, girl," Arden said, tapping the filly's rump. "Be good, now. . . ."

As Glory walked through the doorway, Arden felt her heart breaking. Out in the yard she could see Gramp and Vince Shago. And there by a big limousine with a horse trailer was Tiffany Van Vreen and her aunt.

"There's my Tillie," Tiffany called gaily when she saw Glory coming. "There's my horse!"

"Tillie!" Jesse said in disgust. "What kind of name is that? Her name is Glory."

Tiffany smiled meanly in Arden's direction. "She's *my* horse now," the girl said in a haughty voice, "and I can call her whatever I want. From now on, her name is Tiffany's Tillie!"

Arden couldn't stand it anymore. She ran into the stable, threw herself facedown on a bale of hay, and began to cry. Nothing in the world had ever hurt so much. "It isn't fair!" she sobbed. "Glory's mine! I love her! It isn't fair!"

Through her crying, Arden heard the roar of a car in the driveway. She thought it was probably Tiffany and her aunt leaving with Glory. But a few seconds later Tim was in the stable shaking her shoulder.

"Arden!" he called. "Come on — you've got to get out there. Some guy with a big station wagon and a trailer just drove up. He says that Glory is his! He says she was stolen!"

Arden looked up and wiped her eyes. "Somebody's saying that Glory is stolen?" she said in confusion, as she got up and followed Tim to the doorway. "Who is he?" Tim pointed to an important-looking man in a white cowboy hat.

"He said his name is Jed Wentworth. He's the owner of that big place with all the racehorses — Wentworth Track and Stables!" Tim said.

Arden crept out the door. Her grandparents, Jed Wentworth, and Vince Shago were all standing in a huddle near Glory.

"This is definitely my horse!" Wentworth's voice boomed. "I'd know Rappadan Glory anywhere. She was born at my stable. Her mother is Midnight Clear. See — here are the papers."

Gramp looked at the papers Wentworth was holding. "When I bought the filly at the auction, I was told she'd changed hands a lot," he explained.

Wentworth look disgusted. "Changed hands? I should say so! She was stolen by some fellow who worked for me. When he was afraid the law was going to catch up with him, I reckon he let this filly go to anyone who'd take her!"

Tiffany's aunt stepped up to join the group. "What's going on here?" she demanded. "That's my niece's horse! Mr. Quinn has agreed to give her to me to pay off a debt!"

Wentworth lifted an eyebrow. "Debt? What debt?"

As Thomas Quinn went on to explain about the damaged hedges, Gran came up behind Arden and patted her head. "Don't worry," she said. "Gramp will take care of this."

Meanwhile, Arden noticed that the filly was getting more and more excited — and so was Mrs. Van Vreen!

"I'll pay the thousand dollars!" Mr. Wentworth told Tiffany's aunt, raising his voice. "Don't worry, you'll get your money!"

"Hold on, Mr. Wentworth," Gramp insisted. "Glory may be your horse, but it's my granddaughter who's responsible for the damaged hedges. That debt is something I should pay off."

"I don't care who pays it," Mrs. Van Vreen huffed. "Just make sure it gets paid!"

"But I don't want the money," Tiffany whined at her aunt's elbow. "I want the horse. I want my Tillie!"

Finally everything got ironed out. Mr. Wentworth would pay for the hedges and Gramp would pay him back as soon as he could. But Glory wasn't going to the Van Vreens. Arden couldn't quite understand how it had happened, but Tiffany wasn't getting the horse after all.

But, alas — neither was Arden. Glory was going back to Wentworth Stables.

The Van Vreens had left in a huff and now Jed Wentworth was getting ready to take Glory back.

"All right, everybody, clear the way!" he shouted. "Give us some room to take the horse." Wentworth shook Gramp's hand and thanked him for all he'd done to bring the filly back to health. Then he motioned for his trainer to open the horse trailer. Glory stood alone in the middle of the yard with Joey, who was holding her lead rope.

Arden's lip began to tremble. Glory looked so afraid! "It's all right, girl," Arden whispered. "You're going back to the place where you were born. You'll be all right!"

Wentworth's trainer came over to

Joey, took the rope, and gave it a hard tug. "Let's go, Horsie!" the man said.

Glory snorted and refused to move. The man yanked again. "We're going home now, Rappadan Glory. Let's get out of here!"

Glory reared up on her hind legs and tossed back her jet-black head. "Down!" the man commanded. "Do as you're told! Get into the trailer!" But the frightened horse was beyond hearing.

"Stop it!" Arden cried, running forward. "You're pulling too hard. You don't have to do that."

"Get out of the way, Arden," Gramp shouted. "Watch out for the horse's feet."

But Arden had already grabbed the rope. "It's all right, Glory!" she called with tears streaming down her face. "Calm down — I'm here."

At the sound of Arden's voice, Glory immediately stopped struggling and lowered her feet to the ground. Gramp, Joey, and Vince had all rushed to Arden's aid, but she didn't really need their help. With gentle words and sounds, she soothed the horse. When she finally stopped talking, the filly moved in close to the girl and nuzzled her neck.

Jed Wentworth strode over to Arden. "You handle that horse pretty well," he said.

"My granddaughter has gotten very close to her," Gramp told him.

Wentworth smiled at Arden. "I can see that."

"Do you want me to get Glory into the trailer for you?" Arden asked.

Wentworth hesitated a moment, looking from Arden to Glory, then back again to Arden. "I don't think so," he said slowly.

Then the stable owner turned to Gramp. "How would you like to continue to keep the filly, Mr. Quinn?" he asked. "You could board her here at River Oaks in payment of the debt."

Gramp scratched his thick gray hair

and smiled broadly. "Sounds like a good enough bargain to me. How about you, Arden? What do you think?"

"You mean . . . you mean, we can keep her?" Arden stammered, hardly daring to believe it.

Wentworth patted Glory. "It would be the best thing for the horse — for now, at least. She needs lots of rest and personal attention. You've got a real touch with this animal. If you'd keep working with her, I'd be grateful. What do you say?"

"I say . . . I say, I'd love to!" Arden cried. She threw her arms around Glory. "You hear that, girl? You're going to stay! You're not going anywhere!"

Glory gave Arden a sloppy kiss and everyone laughed.

"Yippee!" Jesse yelled, running over.

"Fantastic!" said Tim.

Gran and Gramp and Joey all looked pleased. Arden was so happy, she thought she'd burst. "Thank you, Mr. Went-

worth," she cried. "Thank you!"

Wentworth cleared his throat. "My pleasure, young lady," he said, tipping his hat. "All the thanks goes to you."

That evening after supper, Gramp invited Arden out for a ride.

"There's a lot of River Oaks you and your filly haven't seen yet," Gramp told her. "I think it's time we did something about that."

"You mean I can bring Glory?" Arden asked excitedly.

Gramp smiled. "Of course. You and that horse are a team now — I've learned that much!"

After they'd saddled up, Arden paused for a moment and looked all around her. The pasture was golden in the sunset, and the sweet sound of birdcalls filled the air. A wave of good feeling washed over her. "Giddyap, Glory," she said softly.

Arden's heart beat excitedly as the

filly moved out. The world was full of adventure, and she was on her very own horse — a horse as black as the night! Taking a deep breath of summer, she raced the wind.